Bring 'em Back Alive!

Capturing Wildlife on Home Video

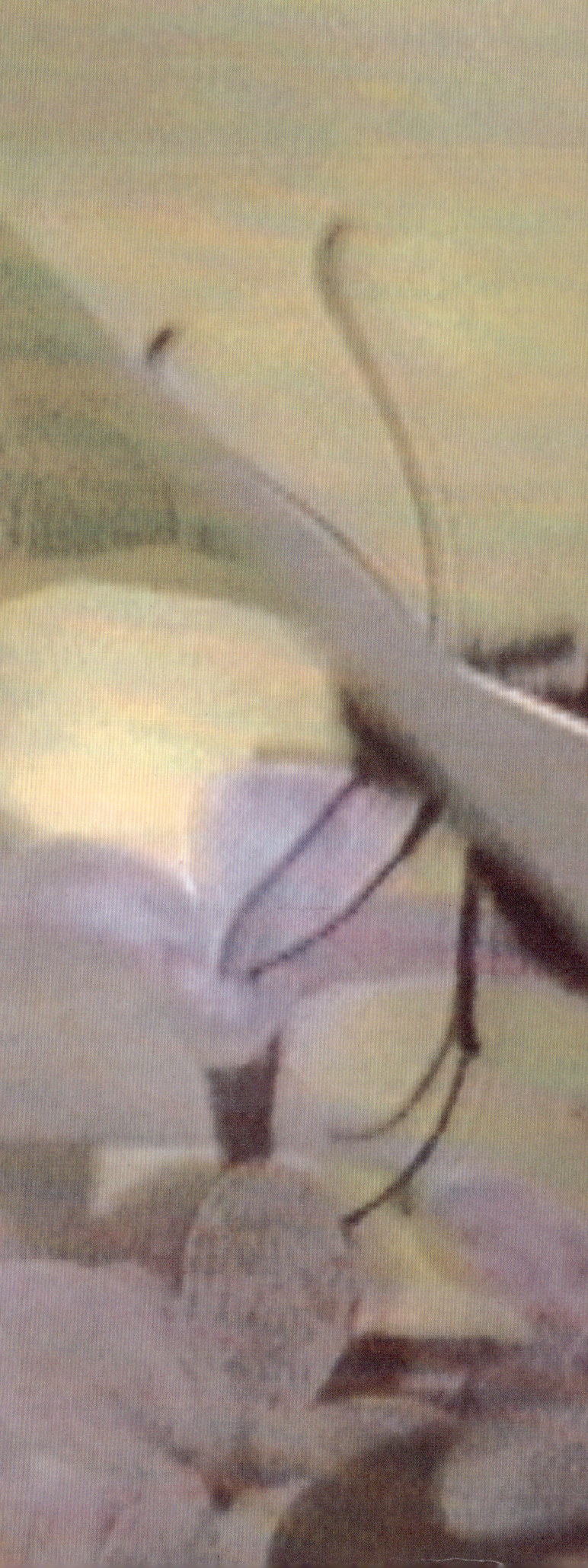

This book is dedicated to my brother Bob, who introduced me to the marvelous medium of 8mm home video

Author's Note

This book was inspired by the many school nature projects that teachers and their students have written to tell me about. It is directed to the countless families and school groups I have seen and met using camcorders to record the sights and sounds at nature centers, wildlife refuges, state parks, and various vacation spots. The activities suggested in this book are intended to be carried out by children under the supervision of adults, to ensure the safety of my young readers, their wildlife subjects, and costly video equipment.

The images in the book are single frames from 8mm videotape (HI-8 format). The author selected each image and "froze" it on a TV monitor, then made a video print using a video printer.

Copyright © 1997 by Jim Arnosky

All rights reserved. No part of this book may be reproduced in any form or by any electronic or mechanical means, including information storage and retrieval systems, without permission in writing from the publisher, except by a reviewer who may quote brief passages in a review.

First Edition

Library of Congress Cataloging-in-Publication Data
Arnosky, Jim.
  Bring 'em back alive! : capturing wildlife on home video / a guide for the whole family by Jim Arnosky. — 1st ed.
    p. cm.
  Summary: Describes how to use a video camera to photograph animals, capturing their individual noises, songs, calls, and actions.
  ISBN 0-316-05105-5 (pb)
  1. Wildlife photography — Amateurs' manuals. 2. Camcorders — Amateurs' manuals. 3. Video recording — Amateurs' manuals.
  [1. Photography of animals. 2. Video recording.] I. Title.
TR727.A76 1997
778.59 — dc20   96-15419

10 9 8 7 6 5 4 3 2 1

IM

Published simultaneously in Canada by Little, Brown & Company (Canada) Limited

Printed in Singapore

Bring 'Em Back Alive!

Capturing Wildlife on Home Video

A Guide for the Whole Family

by Jim Arnosky

Little, Brown and Company
Boston   New York   Toronto   London

Contents

Introduction 6

Video Equipment 9

Telephoto and Safety 13

Portraiture 17

Keeping Your Subject in Frame and in Focus 21

Focusing Through Fence, Shooting Through Glass 25

Wildlife Is Where You Find It 29

Window Feeders 33

Variety 37

Videotaping from a Blind 41

Waiting, Waiting, Waiting for Action 45

Glossary 48

Wood duck

Introduction

In my work as a wildlife artist, I go outside nearly every day to find, sketch, paint, and sometimes photograph animals in their natural habitats. Of all the methods I use in researching wild animals, the one that truly brings 'em back alive is video. Video captures the animals in motion and records their individual noises, calls, and songs, as well as the sounds of the world they live in.

The camcorder is perfectly suited for wildlife photography. Every camcorder can focus on subjects only a few inches away, zoom in on distant subjects, and record in the low light conditions of dawn and dusk, the times when wildlife activity increases.

The color images in this book are single frames taken directly from my own 8mm videotapes. They represent many days afield and many miles of travel to the places where different animals live.

Nothing beats video in capturing the sound and explosive motion of wildlife. I videotaped this alligator sequence from a distance of more than one hundred feet and on the safe side of a state wildlife park fence.

Great horned owl

White-tailed deer

My camcorder has an interchangeable lens system, which gives me optimum telephoto power. However, the images I've chosen for this book could have been obtained or approximated using any home video camcorder.

Join me now as we explore the exciting medium of home video and use every technique it affords to capture on tape elusive wild animals and bring 'em back alive!

*Jim Arnosky
Ramtails 1997*

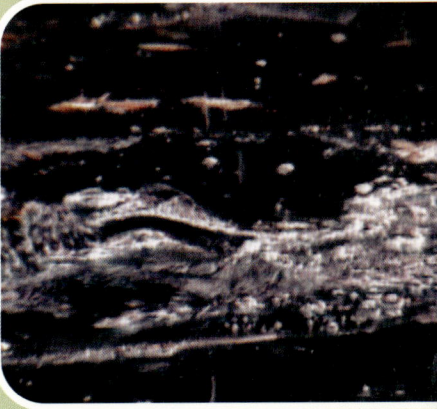

Video Equipment

Video technology advances every year, but the basic tool of videography remains the same: the camcorder. A camcorder is a combination video camera and video cassette player. A camcorder along with a TV to patch into is all you need to videotape and later view your recordings. I use an 8mm camcorder. Other camcorders use larger, full-size VHS cassettes, and some use compact VHS cassettes. Digital camcorders use cassettes that are even smaller than 8mm cassettes. Whichever type of camcorder you have, it can be used for wildlife as long as it has telephoto capability. Most camcorders have zoom lenses, which can bring the image from wide angle to telephoto, at 10X, 12X, or even 20X magnification. All camcorders automatically adjust exposure and focus, and some allow you to switch to manual focus.

Yellowlegs at twilight

Camouflage tape need be applied only to the upper portion of the tripod legs; the telescoping portions are OK as they are.

Camcorders are small and designed to be handheld. Even so, for telephoto taping, I recommend using a tripod whenever possible. In telephoto shots, not only is your subject magnified, but every movement of the camcorder is exaggerated as well. If your hand shakes slightly, the motion will cause your picture to wobble. A sturdy tripod eliminates wobbly pictures.

Since shiny objects tend to alarm wild animals, the best tripods for wildlife are plain black. If your family already has a shiny silver or chrome tripod, you might ask your parents' permission to cover its legs with camouflage tape, which can be found in most hunting supply stores. Get the kind that goes on easily and peels off just as easily. You can also use a patch of camouflage tape to cover the red blinking light on the front of your camcorder. The light is designed to alert people being videotaped that the camera is on. For taping wildlife, the blinking light may be just enough to scare subjects away.

Great egret

Ring-necked pheasant

10

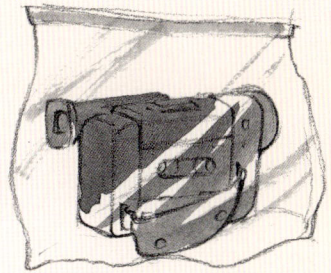

A gallon freezer bag holds most camcorders for transition from cold to warm places.

A camcorder is not fragile, but it should be handled carefully and respectfully. Do not bang or bump it against hard surfaces. Take care to keep it clean and dry. Dampness from rain or even an excessive dewfall can damage the camcorder's electronics or cause it to work poorly. Camcorders work fine in cold weather as long as you keep the battery in a warm pocket up until the time of taping. To avoid accidental spark or shock, be sure to keep the battery terminals from touching any metal objects, such as keys or change. Before bringing a cold camcorder into a warm room or car, wrap it in plastic, and then keep it in the plastic until it warms to room temperature. The plastic prevents condensation (moisture) from forming on or inside the equipment.

Treat the camcorder lens as you would treat your own eyes. Avoid rubbing, scratching, or poking the lens surface. Clean the lens very carefully using delicate lens paper, and never, ever aim the lens directly into the sun.

This video image of a bull moose drinking was taken with a powerful 15X telephoto lens.

Telephoto and Safety

The ultimate goal of any type of wildlife photography is to obtain close-up full-frame pictures of animals without bothering the wildlife or endangering the photographer. The video images in this book of large and especially dangerous animals were all taken from great distances using the telephoto function. What's more, many were taken from the comfort and safety of an automobile, sight-seeing boat, or state-maintained observation platforms, where many other people — children with their parents, retired couples on vacation, other photographers, and supervising park rangers — all shared the wildlife-watching experience. It is important you know that much of the wildlife photography you see is taken under similar circumstances. In no way does it dampen the excitement, challenge the integrity, or lessen the beauty of the pictures and the wild subjects. There is no need to encroach too closely and cause an animal to become nervous, frightened, or defensive.

Bull moose in autumn woods

This ultra-close-up of a garter snake was taken from ten feet away!

Be sure to give endangered or threatened species an extra margin of distance.

Every wild animal — big or small, dangerous or harmless — needs enough space to feel safe and unthreatened. Here are some rules of the road to keep you safe and the wildlife undisturbed. Never corner a wild animal. Do not approach young or baby wild animals — their mothers are surely somewhere nearby. Keep your distance from wild animals that seem tame or unafraid of you. They could be sick and dangerous. Use your zoom lens to bring animals close in your frame. Stay back and watch your subjects up close through your viewfinder. Do not walk while looking through the viewfinder. You can't videotape and watch where you are stepping at the same time. Instead, stand still and videotape with your feet firmly planted on the ground.

Bald eagle

Make a habit of using your zoom. I like to begin a shot wide, showing the animal surrounded by its habitat, then slowly zoom in for a handsome portrait.

Portraiture

Whenever the opportunity to zoom in for a really close portrait presents itself, seize it! This gigantic snapping turtle was resting on the cool grass of our dooryard on its way to the lake when I video-taped its magnificent face. My zoom lens kept me well away from my subject. In fact, the turtle never defensively pulled into its shell, not even slightly. When it began to move again, I stepped out of the way and taped a wide three-quarter-view portrait of its head, neck, shell, and armored forelegs.

*Manatee
at Homosassa Springs
State Wildlife Park*

The secret to good portraiture is waiting for the perfect moment to snap your picture. With video you can stay focused on a subject and keep taping until the perfect pose occurs. I followed this Florida manatee with my lens as it swam just under the surface of the Crystal River. Suddenly the manatee rose and exhaled, sending a spray of water from its nostrils. The pose lasted only seconds, but it was worth waiting for.

Tape everything for at least ten seconds, even relatively still animals. Ten seconds is just enough time for eyes to blink and heads to turn, giving you a moving, breathing portrait. Also, ten seconds is a good long look on a video screen.

Brown pelican

Saw-whet owl

The portraits of the saw-whet owl and red-tailed hawk are of injured birds kept and cared for at a nature center. When you are taping portraits of animals in controlled circumstances, walk slowly around your subject and carefully choose the background — dark or light — before setting up your tripod.

In the wild, you take whatever you can get. I was lucky to capture this blue jay head-on. Songbirds rarely hold their head still for more than a second or two.

Red-tailed hawk

Blue jay

Keeping Your Subject in Frame and in Focus

Using telephoto mode, you can zoom in on a small area with a narrow field of view. Like powerful binoculars, the telephoto function can be used to scan a landscape, one small piece at a time, to look for animals and birds hidden in the scenery. However, the easiest way to spot wildlife is with your own eyes. Before you look through the viewfinder, search for subjects with your naked eyes. Then use a wide angle to create a wide field of view to locate the chosen subject in the lens. Now you are free to let the animal move about in the encompassed scenery, or you can zoom in for close-ups.

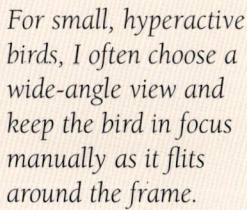

For small, hyperactive birds, I often choose a wide-angle view and keep the bird in focus manually as it flits around the frame.

This mallard with her ducklings called for a steady horizontal pan. To capture a deer drinking, I panned vertically and then zoomed in for a close-up.

Automatic focus works best when you center your subject in the viewfinder. You can also keep an animal in focus by making sure a large part of its body is centered in the frame. If you have a camcorder with the option of manual focus, try switching to it. Let your subject move all around the frame, keeping it in focus by turning the manual focus ring.

Moving your camcorder along with a moving subject is called panning. When panning, keep your camcorder steady and move it in fluid motion in the direction and with the same speed of your subject's movements. If you are using a tripod, loosen the knobs on the tripod head that allow fluid horizontal and

The larger camcorders can be rested on a shoulder for steady panning and shooting without a tripod.

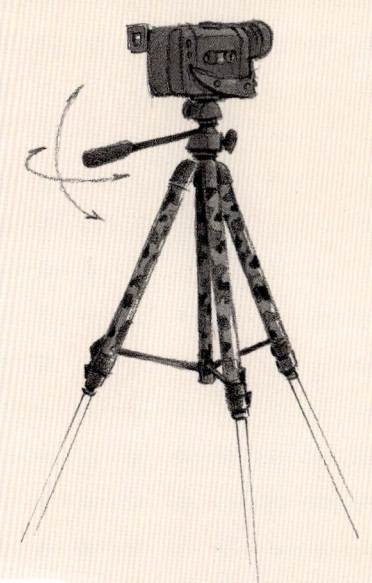

The tripod's panning arm makes it easy to follow your subject as it moves horizontally or vertically.

vertical movement of your camera lens. If your subject is moving slowly, automatic focus will work as you follow the motion with your lens. Fast-moving subjects, such as birds on the wing, may hinder automatic focus and require a switch to manual focus. Never actually follow an animal by running or walking as you videotape. Stand firmly in one spot, and follow your subject's movement with your lens.

At times your subject may suddenly become blurred even though you are keeping it centered in the frame. In most cases, the autofocus is sensing something in front of your subject, a leaf or twig, and focusing on it. You can alleviate this problem by shifting your scene slightly in the frame until the autofocus reads your subject, or by switching to manual focus.

Focusing Through Fence, Shooting Through Glass

The next time your family visits a zoo, aquarium, safari park, or game preserve, take the camcorder along. These places provide perfect opportunities to take intimate telephoto sequences of large, awesome animals that are either extremely dangerous to be near or too elusive to ever be seen in the wild.

A wild school of fish videotaped through the Plexiglas window in an underwater observation area at the Homosassa Springs State Wildlife Park

A permanently injured panther kept and cared for at Homosassa Springs State Wildlife Park

Autofocus works well even through glass, as long as you keep your subjects centered in the frame. Stand a few feet back so your lens is safely away from the glass, and aim your camcorder in a way that keeps your own reflection out of the picture. Zoom in for close-ups. Never tap on aquarium or terrarium glass, and keep your hands off. It disturbs the animals inside.

Your lens can also focus right through wire fencing! Again, stand well back from the fence, and view the scene in wide angle. Then zoom in to the animal behind the fence until you have it fully framed in your viewfinder. Switch to manual focus, and turn the blurry subject into a clear sharp image. That's it! If you don't have the option of manual focus, move the camcorder ever so slightly left, right, up, or down until the autofocus finds its way through an opening in the fence, and as soon as the image sharpens, press RECORD.

I was in a dark room when I videotaped this rattlesnake in its terrarium. In the wide shots, part of my shirt reflected on the glass. But when I zoomed in on the snake's head, it was as if no glass existed.

Wildlife Is Where You Find It

Wherever there is water, food, and shelter, there is wildlife. In fields and small woodlots, residential lawns or city parks, animals can be found by a keen and patient eye. When videotaping in suburban or urban areas, you may choose to show your subjects in man-made environs, or you can show only the wild by carefully choosing your angle of view to eliminate any hint of developed surroundings. Either way is good. Wild animals are interesting and beautiful no matter where they happen to be.

Gulls congregating near a lakeside fast-food restaurant

Leopard frog resting in a lawn puddle

Pigeons are wild birds that make beautiful video subjects.

The first wild moose I ever photographed was munching cabbage in a tiny backyard vegetable garden. In the midst of a blizzard, I sketched a bobcat that had taken refuge from the storm in my neighbor's garage. The cat was resting peacefully on a shelf over a tool bench. Snowy owls are arctic birds. Yet I enjoyed watching and sketching a snowy owl as it perched and flew from place to place on a snow-covered factory roof in the city of Barre, Vermont. To the owl, the great snowfield on the flat roof was very much like arctic tundra. There the white owl, camouflaged against

Believe it or not, these white-tailed deer live in the city — on land surrounding a large industrial plant.

Gecko sunning on a South Carolina park sign

the snow, perched on the roof edge and hunted mice scurrying on the ground below.

Some of my best close-up videography is done right in my backyard — in the flower beds, gardens, and patches of wild grasses that edge the lawns. A short stroll from green place to green place often produces more subjects than can be taped in one afternoon. Spiders, butterflies, caterpillars, slugs, grasshoppers, and crickets show up in every square foot of greenery. The video lens's amazing zoom capability makes it easy to close in on tiny insects six feet away without disturbing them.

For this type of work, use a tripod. When you find a spot buzzing with tiny subjects, set up and stay until you have zoomed in and captured on tape every living creature in range.

If you live in an area where ticks are a problem, wear long pants with the bottoms tucked into your socks. Check yourself for ticks after each video walk. And if you find a tick on your clothing, use a twig or lens brush to brush it off before it can migrate to your skin.

Garden spider

Monarch butterfly

Monarch caterpillar

Window Feeders

Every winter, we try to help our local birds, squirrels, and mice get through the lean cold months by providing seeds, cracked corn, and suet for them to eat. For the shyest winter visitors, we've established a feeding station some distance away from our house near a sheltering tangle of brush and small trees. For bolder individuals, there is a feeder right up against our kitchen window. Such close proximity to wild and hardy little birds is a winter joy, especially to my wife, Deanna, who delights in each newcomer as if it were a special guest.

Most of the time, the birds on the feeder see only a reflection of themselves and their outdoor world in the window glass. Inside, I often can stand my tripod only a few feet from the window and videotape without disturbing them. The telephoto lens makes it possible to reach beyond the window feeder all the way across the yard to the more secluded feeding station. Many beautiful portraits of wild birds are made by professional photographers in exactly this way.

A mix of dry limbs, driftwood, and evergreen boughs nailed to a flat seed feeder

Chickadee

The best feeders for wildlife videography are made of wood — the more weathered, the better. Wood looks more natural in a scene than Plexiglas or metal. But even the most weathered wooden feeders look too tame to really do wildlife subjects justice. To frame our winter visitors in more natural scenery, I tie or tack around each feeder a variety of branches, twigs, and posts for them to climb and perch on.

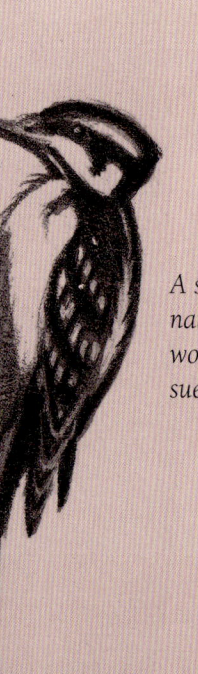

A suet log makes a naturalistic perch for woodpeckers and other suet eaters.

Female cardinal on snowy feeder

Wild animals are creatures of habit. You will find that individuals that come regularly to your feeder will approach it the same way on every visit. They will use the same perches and the same feeding spot, which makes videotaping them easy. Pick an oft-used perch, and focus on it in your viewfinder. The second a subject appears on the perch, press RECORD.

Blue jay

Red squirrel

Variety

With practice, you will be able to keep your subjects in frame and in focus for longer and longer intervals. The longer you can keep your subject in view, the greater variety of movements, lighting, and shading you will record.

Nearly every camcorder lens is surrounded by screw threading, which allows the addition of image-enhancing filters. The simple addition of a haze filter will not only enhance color by cutting through atmospheric haze, but it will also protect the video lens from dust or sand scratches. A polarizing filter enhances blue sky and accents puffy white clouds. A light amber filter produces a warm glow in sunlit scenes.

Rear view of beaver showing how the beaver's tail floats in repose

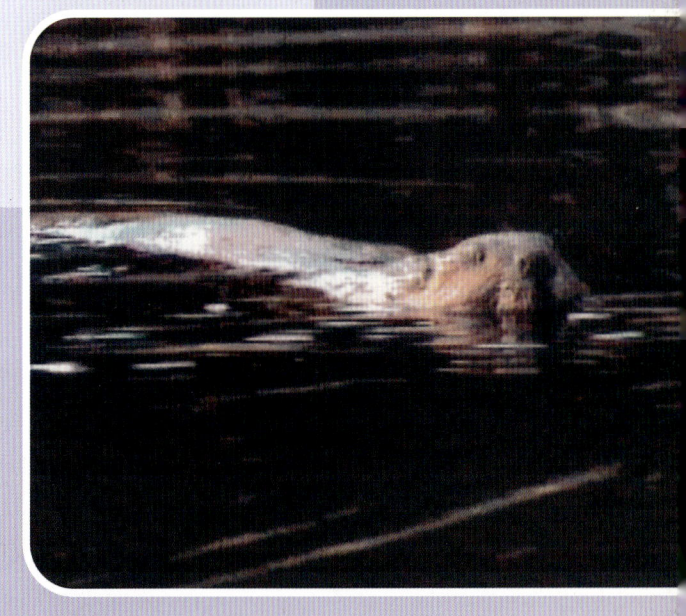

Front view of same beaver recorded only seconds later

Beaver and rippled water

Ruddy duck and water rings

Water and sunlight — a spectacular mix! Whenever these two elements are present, a variety of shapes and hues occur naturally. All you need to do is aim and record; the liquid and light will do the rest. The wildlife subjects on this page are pictured in a world awash with the colors, shapes, and patterns of water and light.

When your subject stands between you and the sun, it is said to be backlit. Because your camcorder automatically adjusts exposure for the brightest light in a scene, backlit subjects appear dark — usually too dark. Many camcorders have a BACKLIT button, which if pressed, will brighten a backlit subject.

Mallard on green water

Canada geese amid horizontal wavelets

You can also brighten backlit subjects by zooming in so that more of the subject's body reads on the camcorder's exposure meter. There are times, however, when backlighting is a most beautiful effect.

When videotaping backlit subjects, be careful never to aim your lens directly into the sun. Direct sunlight can damage a camcorder, and worse, it can cause eye damage. You can keep the sun safely off to an angle and still get the backlight you desire.

Above: Heron, lit from the side
Below: Same heron, backlit after only a slight shift in my camera angle

Note: The heron was taped using an amber filter to warm the scene.

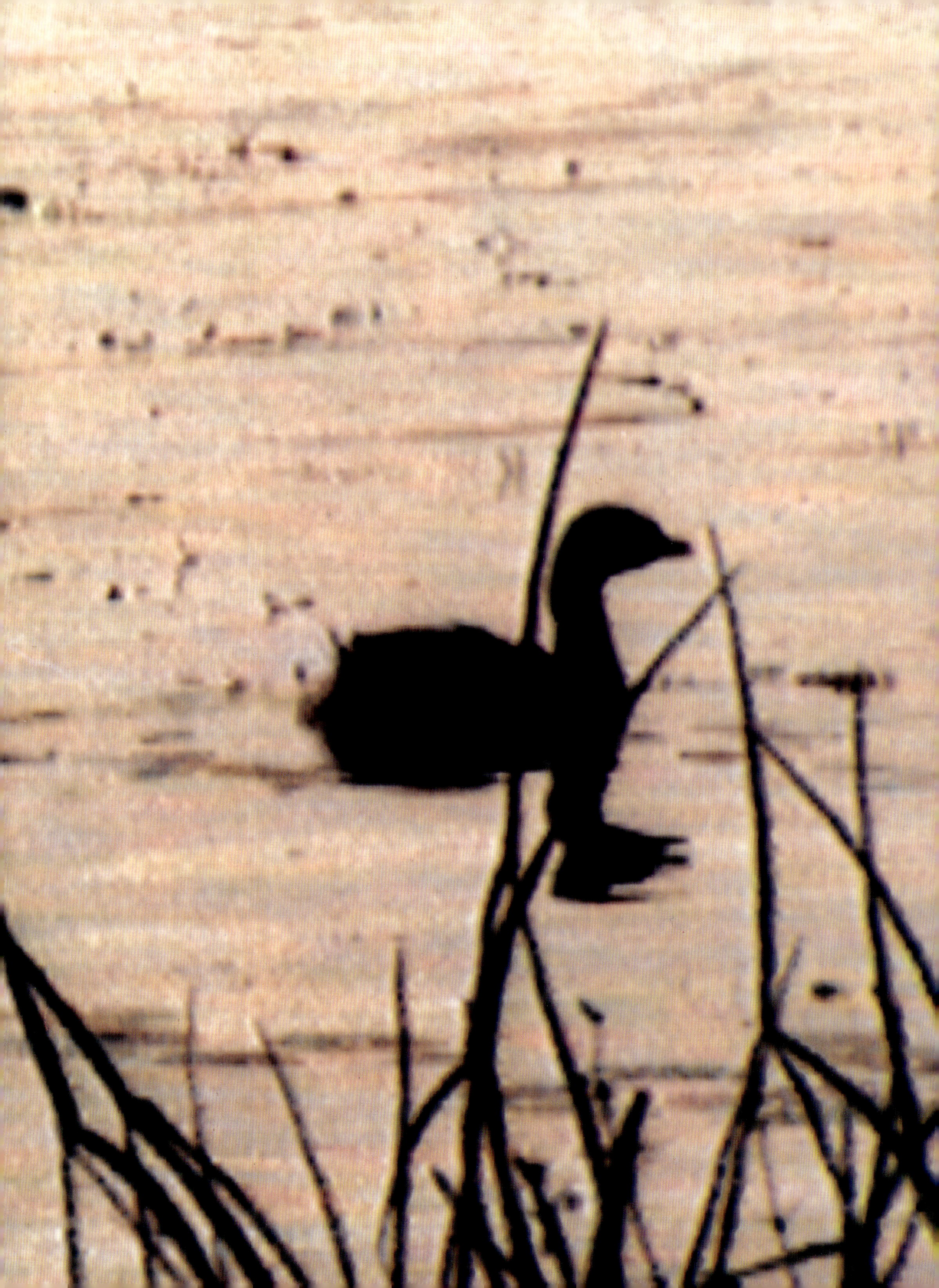

Videotaping from a Blind

If you have a favorite spot where you sit and wait for wildlife, you might see more each visit if you construct a blind to hide inside. The first blind I ever built was on the edge of a broad wild meadow. From my blind, I photographed deer, birds, and any other wild creature that passed by. My blind was simply made— three posts stuck in the ground with burlap stapled to them to form two walls, each with a square window cut out to peek a camera lens through. I use a similar blind today for videotaping. The only change I have made in the original design is a longer, wider window for video panning.

The grebe on the left was videotaped from the shoreline blind shown at right. Note the blind's elongated window, designed for video panning.

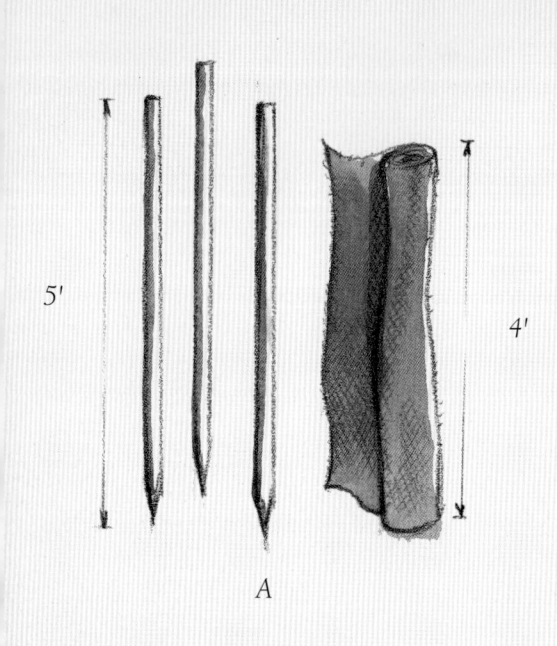

Mallard drake

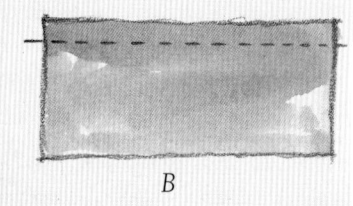

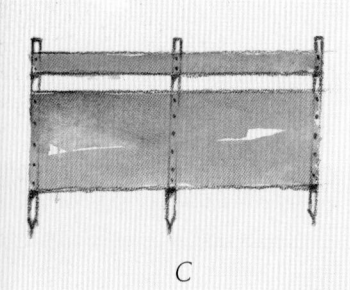

I have had some of my best hours outdoors simply sitting quietly in my blind, awaiting wildlife. The place becomes a world of sounds—birds singing softly in nearby trees, breezes moving through the burlap walls, and the rustling of insects in dry grasses or leaves. Sometimes I bring a pair of earphones, plug into my camcorder's microphone, and listen to the calls of birds far off. When the animal or bird I have been waiting for suddenly arrives, I slowly swivel the camcorder on its tripod, frame the subject in the viewfinder, and press RECORD. (To save battery power, turn your camcorder on only when you want to look or listen with it and, of course, when a subject is in view.)

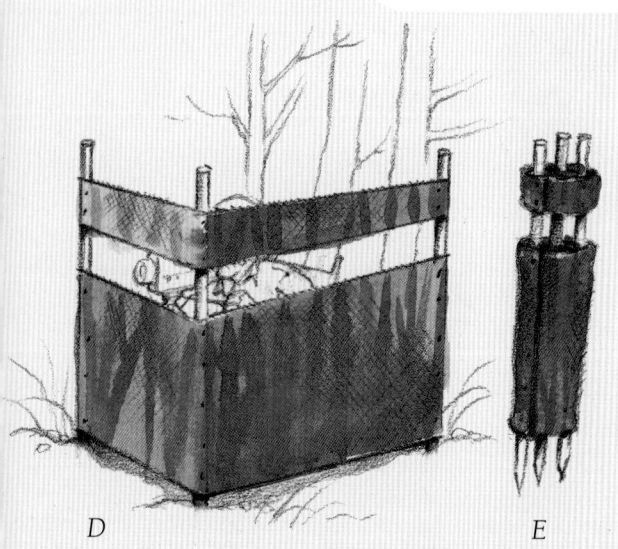

Building a Simple Portable Blind
You will need three 5' stakes and a bolt of burlap cloth 4' by 8' (A). Carefully cut a 6" strip off the top of the cloth (B). Tack or staple burlap to stakes as shown (C). Set up the blind by pounding the stakes into the ground. Crouch or sit behind the burlap walls (D). Roll up the blind tightly for easy carrying (E).

Great blue heron

Dragonfly

After your blind has been set up awhile, the local wildlife will accept it as their own. Small animals will perch, scurry, and burrow around, on, and in it. The close-ups on this page were all taken of animals sharing my blind with me.

Ruddy turnstone

Swallowtail butterfly

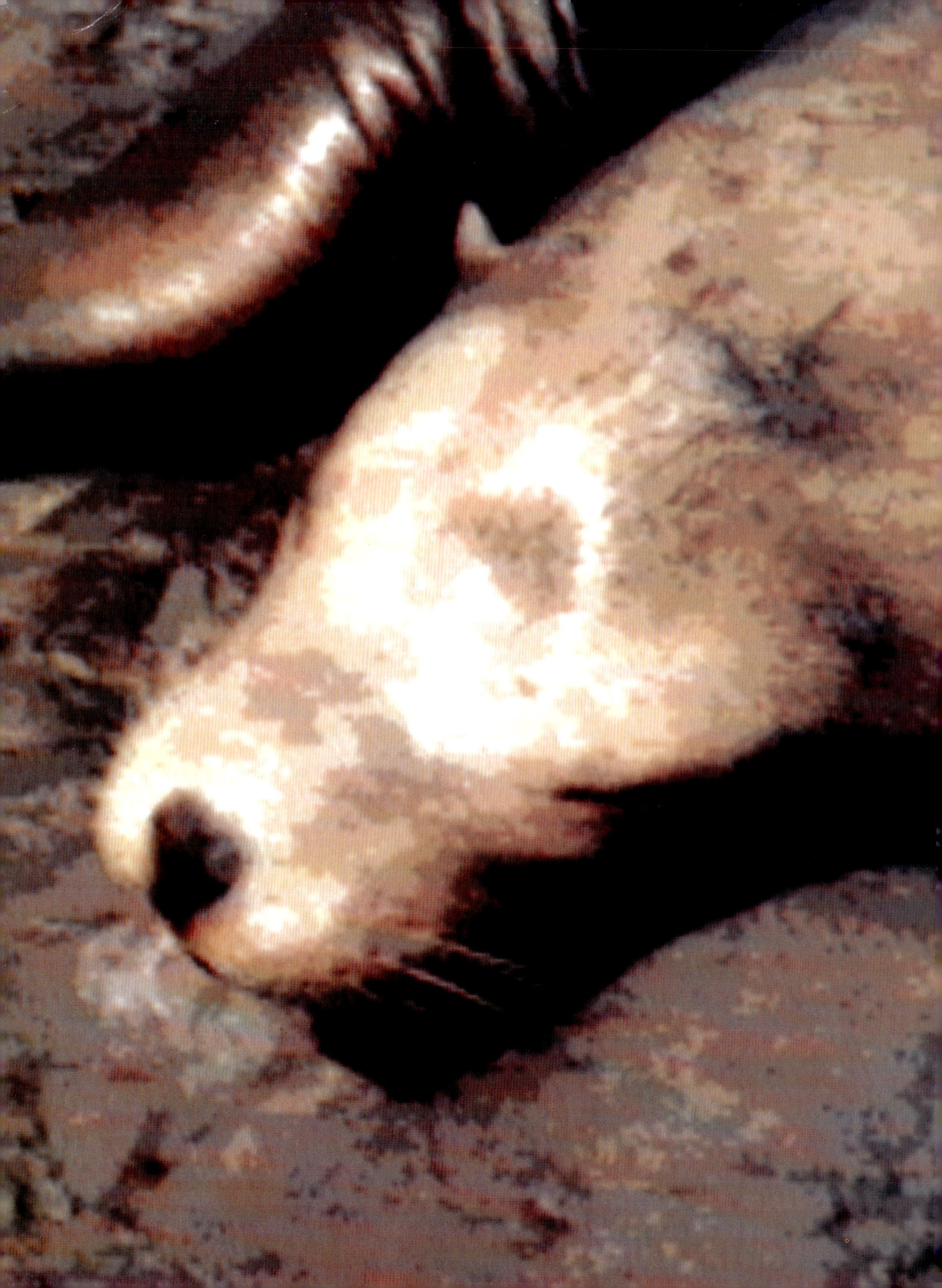

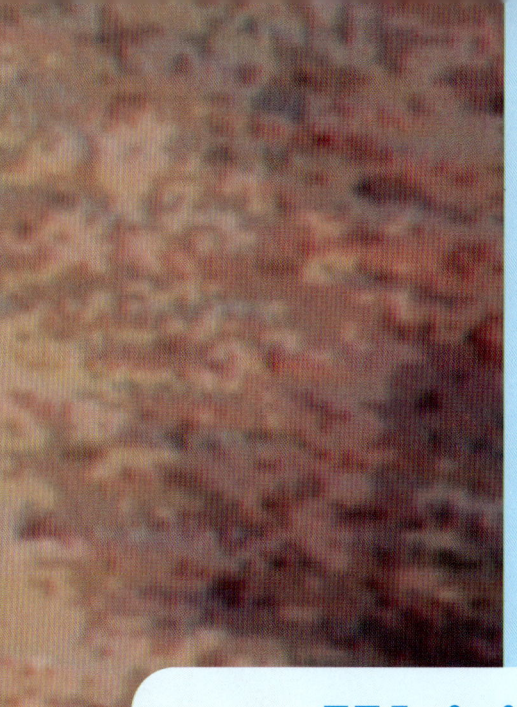

Waiting, Waiting, Waiting for Action

Any kind of wildlife photography involves a lot of waiting—waiting for wildlife to come to your blind, waiting for a subject to turn and strike a good pose, waiting for the light to be just right. Wildlife videography also includes waiting for action. Once you have an animal in your lens, there is no guarantee the animal will move. Wild animals spend a large portion of their time simply resting. I have waited more than an hour for a turtle resting on a trail to take its next step. I once waited fruitlessly for a sleeping beaver to awaken before I finally packed up and left the beaver still snoozing away on the riverbank.

Of course some tape of an animal in repose is better than no recorded image at all. But a still subject is essentially a still picture, and in video you want action! However, the action should come naturally. As tempting as it may be to do something to make static wildlife move for video footage, you should never do so.

Patience has its rewards. After I waited one late winter afternoon for this otter to emerge from a long dive, it not only finally emerged, but it also crawled out of the cold water onto the ice.

I once waited, lens focused on one particularly lovely lily, for a hummingbird flitting around from lily to lily to fly to mine. When the tiny bird finally zipped into view, it lingered. I have every wing beat captured on tape.

Two successive video frames of a hovering hummingbird

An aquatic animal's exit is often more dramatic than its entrance.

Capturing images of wildlife acting naturally in their natural surroundings is an activity you'll never outgrow. I've been at it for more than half my life, and I still eagerly anticipate the next outing. Each time I return with new video footage, I view and re-view the tape, studying every sound and movement, reliving moment by moment the whole wonderful experience.

Glossary

Backlit: When a subject is between the camera and the light source

Blind: A structure in which to hide, in order to observe and videotape wildlife

Camcorder: A small portable combination video camera and videocassette recorder

Full frame: When a subject viewed through a camera lens fills the entire picture area

Habitat: The place where particular animals or plants live

Panning: Moving your camera slowly horizontally or vertically, usually to follow the motion of your subject

Patch: To electronically link camcorder and TV in order to watch your video on television

Portrait: A close-up of a subject's head and/or torso

Telephoto: Magnification of subjects at a distance

Tripod: A three-legged adjustable stand used to support a camera

Viewfinder: The small black-and-white or color video monitor inside a camcorder eyepiece

Zoom: To either quickly or smoothly and gradually change from wide angle to close-up; a lens with this capability

10X, 12X, 20X, etc.: Various powers of magnification in zoom or telephoto lenses; 10X, for example, indicates that the subject appears ten times closer than it actually is